Animal friends

Catherine and Laurence Anholt

little ORCHARD

Have *you* got a pet to hold?

Tortoises can creep and crawl.

Feed the birds, it's very cold.

Slimy snails up on a wall.

I am running with my dog.

I am hopping like a frog.

Flitter, flutter, fly away.

Can we feed the ducks today?

I can climb up on a gate.

Stop, please car, you'll have to wait.

Ladybirds are red and small.

On a horse I'm very tall.

Four fat puppies, aren't they funny?

Would you like to stroke my bunny?

This pink pig is very fat.